For my longtime agent and friend, Laura Blake Peterson.
— J.G.

For my parents, Liang and Jenny, and also my little sister, Ariel.
Thank you for the never-ending love and support.
— M.L.A.

Text copyright © 2021 Jeff Gottesfeld
Illustrations © 2021 Michelle Laurentia Agatha

Cover and internal design by Simon Stahl

Library of Congress Control Number: 2021930927

Published by Creston Books, LLC
www.crestonbooks.co

ISBN 978-1-939547-94-1
Source of Production: 1010 Printing
Printed and bound in China
5 4 3 2 1

The Christmas Mitzvah

By Jeff Gottesfeld

Illustrated by
Michelle Laurentia Agatha

Al Rosen was a Jewish man who loved Christmas. It wasn't his holiday. He had Hanukkah, the Festival of Lights. But what could be bad about peace on earth and goodwill to humanity?

On a Hanukkah night that was also Christmas Eve, Al and his son Jonathan kindled their menorah and then walked through the neighborhood to admire the decorations.

At Clarence's corner newsstand, the clerk shivered in the cold.

"Merry Christmas, Clarence! Why aren't you with your family?"

"Boss wants me here 'til midnight," Clarence groused.

Al shook his head. His friend should not have to work on Christmas Eve. "Go home. Let us finish your shift. Call it a Christmas mitzvah."

"A mitz-who?"

Jonathan explained. "A mitzvah. A good deed. But also a commandment. What God wants."

Clarence nodded. "I get it. Anyone can do a mitzvah." Then he frowned. "Even if the Good Lord wants it, you two can't run a newsstand."

"Give Him a hand," Al said with a grin. "Teach us."

The Rosens ran the newsstand for several Christmas Eves. But when Jonathan went away to college and Clarence moved on, Al had nothing to do on Christmas Eve.

He called a radio station. The DJ put him on the air.

"Merry Christmas, everybody. I'm Al Rosen. I'm Jewish. If you're Christian and have to work tonight but would rather be with your family, I'll do your job. For nothing."

The switchboard lit up red and green.

For thirty more years, Al did Christmas mitzvahs.
He pumped gas,
        lugged bags,

tended bar,

spun records,

and changed bedpans.

Some jobs he did better than others.

Al bagged groceries,

took tolls,

sorted mail,

filed papers,

and parked cars.

Jonathan became a doctor and moved back to town.
Together they mucked stalls,
collected eggs,
exercised dogs,
fed cats,
and scrubbed cages.

Al became a grandfather when Jonathan married Beth, and Sarah was born. Then Ari. And Zack. In wind, sleet, and chill, the Rosens bundled up.

To change tires,
direct traffic,
sweep sidewalks,
deliver parcels,
and plow snow.

The mitzvahs became local legend.
Bussing tables,
   peeling potatoes,
      pouring coffee,
         washing dishes,
            and mopping floors.

Years piled up like drifts in a blizzard. Al grew gray and achy. Yet come Christmas Eve, he'd find his parka and head into the night.

To guard gates,

open doors,

answer phones,

do laundry,
and shine shoes.

Inspired by Al and Jonathan, Christian and Muslim friends did their jobs on the Jewish High Holidays.

The idea spread. People volunteered on each other's special days. Some jobs they did better than others.

One Christmas Eve brought a bittersweet story on the local news.

    "A Christmas miracle ends this snowy evening. Thirty-six years ago tonight, a Jewish man took on the work of a newsstand clerk and sent the fellow home for the holiday. Al Rosen kept up that tradition for more than three decades, learning dozens of jobs to let strangers have the night with their families. He says he's finally too old for his annual 'Christmas Mitzvah.' Al, if you're listening, thank you for a job well done and a life well lived. And Happy Hanukkah."

Jonathan's phone buzzed all day. There were whispered conversations. As dusk approached, Al decided there was too much snow to see the lights. Plus, he was so tired.

"We still need to light the menorah," said Sarah.

As she was about to strike a match, the doorbell rang.

"Why don't you get it, Dad?" Jonathan asked.

Al shuffled to the door.

No one was there.

But the driveway and walkways were shoveled. A family of new snowmen grinned charcoal smiles. And a snowplow flashed yellow lights at the far end of a blue-and-white carpet.

A banner hung from the plow.

Out stepped Clarence, bundled against the cold.
And a gas station attendant,
bellhop,
bartender,
DJ,
and nurse's aid.

Grocery bagger, toll taker, mail sorter, file clerk, and babysitter.
Stable hand, egg farmer, dog walker, shelter aide, and lab tech.
Tire changer, traffic cop, sidewalk sweeper,
delivery man, and snowplow driver.

Busboy, short order cook, waitress, dishwasher, and janitor.
Guard, doorman, receptionist, laundromat attendant, and shoeshine guy.
Plus, their families.
All the folks easy to dismiss in a world that mistakes wealth for worth.

Now old himself, Clarence led the group. "We want to thank you, Al. For the gift of Christmas."

The snowplow driver offered Al his keys. "Come on. We've got streets to clear and decorations to see."

Al stared out at a life well lived and wished he had one more mitzvah in him.

He did.

"Come in, everyone," he called. "It's Hanukkah. Let's light the menorah."

Clarence looked puzzled. "But we're not Jewish."

Al laughed. "You said it yourself, Clarence: anyone can do a mitzvah!"

Behind a picture window, on a street of brightly lit homes, a throng of God's children marveled at the shimmer of glowing candles.

Author's Note

In Milwaukee, Wisconsin in 1969, a Jewish man named Al Rosen met a Christian man who said sadly that he'd have to miss Christmas Eve with his family due to work obligations. Rosen was so moved by the man's story that he called a radio station. He got the disc jockey to announce that he would be willing to take over the work of a Christian stranger on Christmas Eve, so that the Christian could celebrate with his family. The response was overwhelming. That Christmas Eve, Rosen filled in as the bartender at a corner tavern. He became a local legend as he continued his tradition for several decades. He worked as a hospital orderly, convenience store clerk, hotel bellman, and more, and inspired people of faith around the world to take the jobs of others on their holy days. His streak of mitzvahs ended only with his death at age 80.

For more about the real Al Rosen, visit www.crestonbooks.co/christmasmitzvah.

The joyful, eight-day Jewish holiday of Hanukkah celebrates the rededication and relighting of the sacred oil lamp in the Jewish Temple in Jerusalem more than two thousand years ago, after a military victory. It is marked by the progressive illumination of a nine-branched menorah, the *dreidel* spinning top game, and traditional foods often fried in oil. Long a minor festival on the Jewish calendar, it has grown in significance and meaning because of its timing at Christmas season. For more about Hanukkah: www.myjewishlearning.com/article/hanukkah-101.

About the Author and Illustrator

Jeff Gottesfeld writes for page, stage, screen, and television. He has won many awards, including ones from the American Library Association, the Association of Jewish Libraries, and the Writer's Guild. *The Tree in the Courtyard: Looking Through Anne Frank's Window* was named a *New York Times* Best Illustrated Children's Book. His latest book with Creston is *No Steps Behind: Beate Sirota Gordon's Battle for Women's Rights in Japan.* You can read more about him at www.jeffgottesfeldwriter.com.

Michelle Laurentia Agatha was born in Jakarta, Indonesia. Since she was young, she has always had a huge interest in cartoons and illustrated books. Michelle pursued her dream to become an illustrator by earning a Bachelor of Fine Arts degree from the Academy of Art University in San Francisco. Currently, Michelle is working as a children's book illustrator, concept artist, and graphic designer. *The Christmas Mitzvah* is her first book.